ISBNs

Paperback: 978-1-80227-249-9

Ebook: 978-1-80227-250-5

Luke & The Ghost Dog

For Max - Who will be with us forever.

Luke blearily opened his eyes. He could smell the sea air and hear the gulls calling from his open bedroom window. Perhaps if his mum had the time, he, Mum and his best friend Ben could take Max to the beach after school today.

One of the reasons they had bought their house was because it was so close to the beach and on a fine day, Luke could just see the sea from his bedroom window. Max loved the beach, digging in the sand and jumping in the waves. It always made Luke chortle. When they had first got Max, they had mistaken him for a seal when he swam out to them and Luke had nearly jumped out of the sea in panic. The whole family still laughed at this memory.

When he was young, Max had been the funniest jet-black Labrador. His stumpy legs and huge paws had been comical at first, but over the years, Luke had stopped noticing those things.

Luke peered onto his bedroom floor and then the memory engulfed him like waves crashing on the shore. Wave followed after wave as he realised that Max was gone forever.

Mum had tried to explain that he had lived to be a very old dog and that twelve was a good age. She had gone on to say that in dog years, that was eighty-four and lots of dogs don't live that long. Luke suddenly felt the tears brimming in his eyes as he thought about all of the days ahead without Max. He understood what his mum had said but it just did not feel right. Max had loved to play catch and hide-and-seek with Luke, but as he got older, the games got shorter and the rests in between got longer.

Luke dragged himself out of bed, wiped the tears from his eyes and trudged down the stairs reluctantly. He knew he would see an empty bed by the table and an empty collar hanging by the door.

Luke's mum tried to be cheerful when he arrived at the kitchen door but it was hard for her too. After all, they had got Max when he was young and he had been a treasured member of the family ever since then.

"Come on, Luke, you should have some breakfast and then you need to get ready for school," she said brightly.

"Dad had to leave early but I can drop you off this morning. Are you alright to walk home after school?"

"Yes," responded Luke dejectedly.

"Remember to take the safe way home. No shortcuts along the cliff path!"

Luke finished his breakfast, lost in his own thoughts. The world, usually so full of colour, wagging tails and warmth, felt grey, bleak and joyless.

In the school playground, the gang of boys who teased Luke started as soon as he walked through the school gate. Frank was always the worst and Luke never understood what had happened between them. He had been one of Luke's friends in their last school, and, along with Ben, the three boys had been inseparable. However, Frank had found new friends now and had started to torment Luke. Ben's big brother and Frank's big brother were friends and they told Ben that Frank thought their games were too silly and that they needed to grow up!

Sometimes Frank and his gang surrounded Luke and took it in turns to call him names. At other times, they would even push him.

Usually, Ben stood up for Luke and always told Frank to leave them both alone. However, Ben was off sick today, so Luke knew he was on his own. Today, however, Luke just did not care. His heart was engulfed with sadness and he didn't hear the words the boys were saying.

The boys were always too clever to get caught by the teachers and Luke and Ben never said anything. Instead, they dreamed up plots to get the gang back for what they were doing. When the bell went, Luke plodded into class and hunkered down in his chair. Thankfully, Frank and his gang left him alone for the rest of the day and for Luke, time passed in a blur.

Luke regretted taking the shortcut home as soon as he started to carefully pick his way along it. The cliff path Luke's mum had warned him about was narrow and close to the edge. It was crumbly underfoot and he skidded on the stones. He realised that he should have listened to his mum's warning. He just wanted to talk to Ben and then curl up in a tiny, insignificant ball on his bed. His sadness was like an avalanche engulfing him.

He had gone some way along the path when he heard familiar voices behind him. Not today, he thought. Why can't they just leave me alone?

If Ben was with him, they would laugh and make a game of hiding or running, but today, he just didn't have the energy and he didn't care.

"Here he is, boys," jeered Frank. "Let's have some fun!"

The boys started to push Luke around, unaware that the particular part of the path they were standing on was sloped and was even looser because it was so close to the cliff edge. Suddenly, Luke stumbled and lost his footing. With a gasp, he started to scrabble around on the path, his feet slipping underneath him.

The stones gave way and Luke could feel himself tumbling, tumbling down and down, the wind whooshing past him. He landed suddenly with a jolt on a ledge on the side of the cliff.

Luke sat up and dusted himself off. The ledge was narrow and uncomfortable, but just wide enough if he sat still.

He checked himself all over and knew he was not hurt, but when he peered up, his heart sank. He had fallen really far and there was no way he could climb back up the cliff.

He peeped timidly over the edge. Below, all he could see were crashing waves and monstrous rocks. Worse than all of this, though, he knew that his mum was going to be furious with him for taking the shortcut home. He sat with his head in his hands, trying to control the overwhelming sadness and fear, when suddenly, he felt something cold pushing at his fingers.

"Where's that coming from?" There it was again! He looked around but couldn't see anything. Then he felt a familiar warm muzzle and soft, silky ears. It felt like a dog but the only dog he knew was Max, and he was gone!

There was the feeling again! The wet, cold nose and this time, it was followed by a whimper and a gentle bark.

"Max," laughed Luke, "is it really you?"

A ghostly bark responded again.

Luke immediately felt safe and reassured.

He didn't know how he knew it was Max; perhaps it was just a feeling. Everything would be alright if Max was here. The next thing he knew he was hugging that familiar, trusted, warm dog body. Oh, how he knew and loved this dog.

"Max, you have to go and get help," Luke whispered bravely.

Then Max, the invisible ghost dog, gave a long, loud, ear-splitting and earth-shattering howl and was gone. Luke hugged his knees to his chest and knew that his ghostly friend would not let him down.

Back up on the cliff path, Frank and the gang were already feeling very sick at the thought of what they had done. The second they were about to speak, they all heard the ghostly howl.

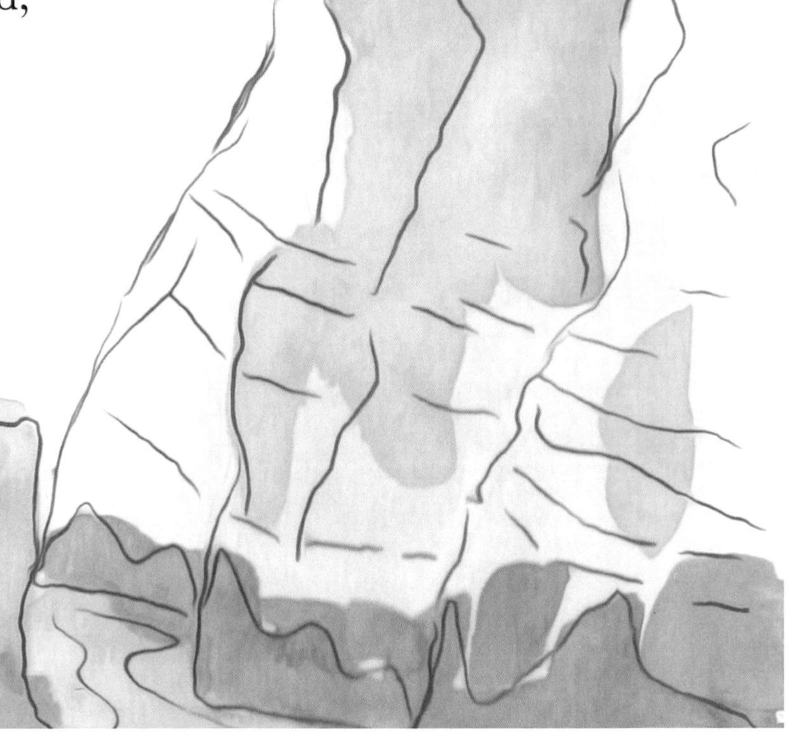

The boys looked at each other in horror.

“Let’s get out of here!” they all squealed in unison, but before they could move, they heard a quiet, ghostly sound.

“Grr,” a noise whispered in the breeze right next to them.

“Grrr,” there it was again.

“Grrrr!” It was louder now, so the boys could all hear it.

“What was that?” whispered Frank faintly.

The boys were rooted to the spot in terror. They all began babbling and feeling even more petrified than before.

Summoning up their remaining courage, the boys scuttled away as fast as rockets, not thinking to stay and help Luke.

Luke's mum always had busy days at work. She arrived home that day feeling exhausted but looking forward to seeing Luke. She had been distracted all day worrying about him. She knew that today would have been difficult for Luke because of Max. She knew how close Luke and Max had been; inseparable really, always together having fun. Max would leave a big hole in their lives.

Just as she got out of the car and turned around, she heard a frantic bark. She looked around but couldn't see where it was coming from. How odd, she thought. Then she heard it again, but this time, it was right next to her and made her jump! She felt something cold and wet in her hand.

"What on earth is going on?" she exclaimed loudly.

The next thing she knew, she had landed on her back, bowled over by an invisible force. She lay there for a moment, stunned and bewildered. Suddenly, she felt like she was being licked, and in between licks, she heard barking - but there was no dog! Instinctively, she knew that this presence was Max and that something was wrong, she was sure of it.

She got up quickly and ran into the house.

"Luke, Luke! are you there?" she called. No reply.

The barking continued.

“Luke!” she shouted. The barking got louder.

“Luke, answer me!” she screamed, panicking by this time.

The barking was frantic now and had reached fever pitch and Luke’s mum knew that she had to find Luke.

“Max, where is he?”

A wet, cold feeling in her hand...a nose? She grabbed her phone from her bag. The wet feeling disappeared and a furry, warm body replaced it. Gingerly, she wrapped her arms around the invisible yet familiar shape and held on. Max gave a whine of encouragement.

Slowly, the ghost dog started to lead her towards the cliff path. After a while, she began to realise where they were going, and the feeling of panic and dread grew even stronger inside her.

“Oh Max,” she said. “What has happened?”

An encouraging yip gave her a little reassurance.

Luckily, they didn’t pass anyone on their short journey to the cliff path. It would have looked rather odd, a woman with her arms wrapped around thin air, talking to herself!

It felt like it took forever to reach the path, but it actually only took a few minutes with her sure-footed companion guiding her.

“Help, help, someone, down here!” Luke’s mum heard the cries whispering on the breeze from down below. Was that Luke’s voice?

The ghost dog started to bark and howl.

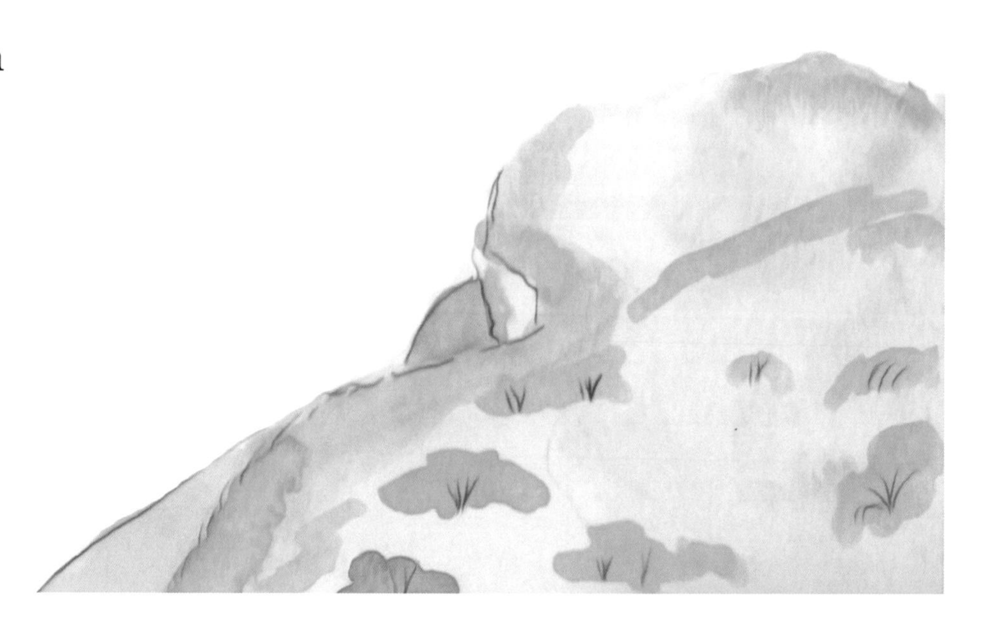

"Max, is that you?" came a cry from below.

By this time, Luke's mum had reached the edge of the cliff and could see how the path had been disturbed and had slipped away.

"Luke!" she cried, peering over the side of the cliff.
The ghost dog howled.

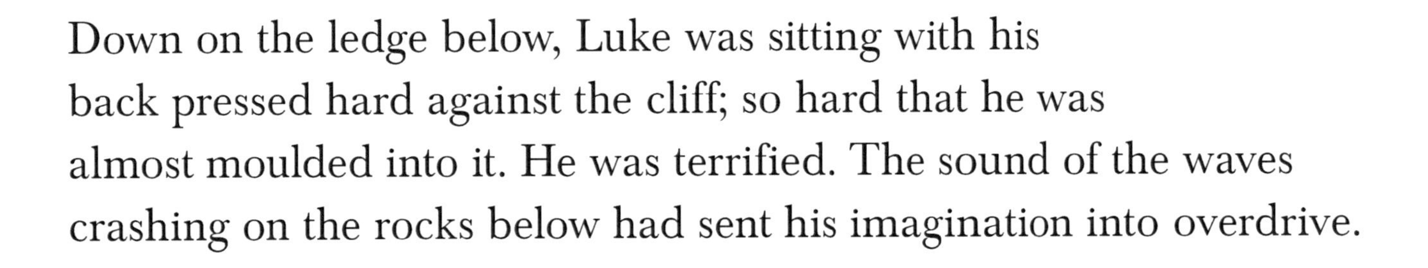

Down on the ledge below, Luke was sitting with his back pressed hard against the cliff; so hard that he was almost moulded into it. He was terrified. The sound of the waves crashing on the rocks below had sent his imagination into overdrive.

Suddenly, he felt a cold, wet nose press into his hand again. Then he felt an invisible, furry body press up against him reassuringly. He felt the familiar weight of a head in his lap. He stroked the ghost dog's head and ruffled his ears.

He felt safe again.

"Max, I love you so much," said Luke. He wasn't sad anymore but he wasn't sure he would be able to explain why.

A comforting whine of encouragement emanated from the dog.

Luke's mum had telephoned the rescue services who had just arrived. It didn't take long for the rescue team to winch Luke back to safety. He hadn't been hurt when he fell, just badly scared, but his ghostly friend had helped with that.

"You are a very lucky young man!" exclaimed the rescue chief.

"I will have to write my report about how it happened."

"It was an accident," said Luke. "Honestly, I was running and I accidentally got too close to the edge and I slipped. Then the cliff gave way."

Luke heard a very quiet whine on the breeze.

"Sshh," he whispered.

"Are you sure that's what happened, Luke?" his mum asked incredulously.

WOOOF !
WOOOOOOF !

"Yes, Mum; totally positive."

There was that whine again, followed by a menacing growl.

"Sshhh," whispered Luke again. "I have a plan."

Back at home, Luke's mum fussed over him. Explaining it all to Luke's dad took a long time, but neither Luke nor his mum mentioned their mysterious ghostly encounter. Luke's mum made his favourite tea and even suggested that he stay at home from school the next day to rest after his terrible ordeal.

Later, in bed that night, cuddled up to his ghostly friend, Luke whispered quietly in his ear, and, if dogs could laugh, you would have heard a great bellow of laughter. As it was, he whined quietly in Luke's ear to show that he understood.

Over at Frank's house, all was quiet. Frank had decided to go to bed early. He was still trying to work out what he had heard on the cliff and, although he had found out that Luke was safe, he was terrified that he would be in trouble for his part in the 'accident'.

He was lying there with the covers pulled tightly up around his neck when he heard a soft growling sound next to him.

Oh no, not again!" he shuddered.

The growling got a bit louder and this time it was right next to his ear. Frank started to tremble. He pulled the covers up over his head but the minute he did that, the growling turned into a hushed but distinct howl. Slowly but surely, the covers were then dragged down over the foot of his bed and as this happened, the covers took on the shape of a dog's body as though they were draped over a real dog!

"Mum!" he screeched, running from his bedroom in terror.

That evening, Max, the ghost dog, visited every member of the gang in turn, doing exactly the same thing to each of them as he had done to Frank. By the time he had finished visiting the last of the boys, they were all deeply regretting their actions that day.

Back at his house, Luke, with his arms wrapped tightly around his ghostly friend, chuckled softly into his pillow. That night, his dreams were once again full of colour and warm, familiar smells; dreams of running on the beach with Max and his best friend Ben, swimming in the sea and making plots and plans.

Suddenly, he couldn't wait for tomorrow and the new adventures it would bring with Max, his ghost dog.

Lightning Source UK Ltd.
Milton Keynes UK
UKRC030948070222
398309UK00001B/7